Violet thumped her fists against the door while Twinkle hit it with his hooves, but it held firm. Eventually, they sank back, exhausted. "What are we going to do?" Violet cried. "We've got to get out of here and warn the others."

★ ★ ★

LOOK OUT FOR MORE ADVENTURES AT

★ ⋆ ★

UNICORN ★ ACADEMY

Violet and Twinkle

JULIE SYKES

illustrated by LUCY TRUMAN

A STEPPING STONE BOOK™
Random House 🏠 New York

Text copyright © 2019 by Julie Sykes and Linda Chapman
Cover art and interior illustrations copyright © 2019 by Lucy Truman

All rights reserved. Published in the United States by Random House Children's Books, a division of Penguin Random House LLC, New York. Originally published in paperback in the United Kingdom by Nosy Crow Ltd, London, in 2019.

Random House and the colophon are registered trademarks and A Stepping Stone Book and the colophon are trademarks of Penguin Random House LLC.

Visit us on the Web! rhcbooks.com

Educators and librarians, for a variety of teaching tools, visit us at RHTeachersLibrarians.com

Library of Congress Cataloging-in-Publication Data
Names: Sykes, Julie, author. | Truman, Lucy, illustrator.
Title: Violet and Twinkle / Julie Sykes ; illustrated by Lucy Truman.
Description: First American edition. | New York : Random House Children's Books, 2021. | Series: Unicorn Academy ; 11 | "A Stepping Stone Book." | Summary: Violet, Twinkle, and their friends embark on an adventure across a frozen lagoon, but this fun outing takes a sinister turn, impelling Twinkle to discover his magic so he can lead them to a daring rescue.
Identifiers: LCCN 2020031190 (print) | LCCN 2020031191 (ebook) | ISBN 978-0-593-30785-4 (trade pbk.) | ISBN 978-0-593-30786-1 (lib. bdg.) | ISBN 978-0-593-30787-8 (ebook)
Subjects: CYAC: Unicorns—Fiction. | Magic—Fiction. | Boarding schools—Fiction. | Schools—Fiction.
Classification: LCC PZ7.S98325 Vi 2021 (print) | LCC PZ7.S98325 (ebook) | DDC [Fic]—dc23

Printed in the United States of America
10 9 8 7 6 5 4 3 2 1
First American Edition

For Mrs. MacNish and all at
Kincardine-in-Menteith Primary

CHAPTER 1

Violet and her unicorn, Twinkle, stood very still as the tiger circled them. It looked right at Violet, a growl rumbling in its throat. Violet knew it was only Pearl, Matilda's unicorn, using a glamour—an illusion—but it looked just like a real tiger, and she couldn't hold back her shriek as the tiger pounced. But then she heard Matilda's giggle, and just like that the tiger faded—its paws turning into hooves and its stripy tail becoming pink and yellow. Violet grinned as the tiger's last whisker disappeared, leaving Matilda and Pearl in its place.

"Wow! That was great, Matilda! Pearl looked so

fierce. I really thought she was going to eat us," said Violet.

Twinkle nodded, adding, "It was very good, even though I could see bits of Pearl's mane showing through the glamour at the end."

Pearl frowned. Matilda gave her a hug. "Doing a glamour is really hard. It takes a lot of magic to keep it going. I think you were amazing, Pearl."

"Me too," said Violet, shooting a look at Twinkle. She knew he didn't mean to be unkind, but sometimes he just said what he thought without realizing how it might sound. She did love him, but she found his bluntness pretty embarrassing at times. She was the complete opposite of him—she really hated hurting people's feelings.

Nearby, the rest of Diamond dorm were practicing their magic too. Honey, Freya's unicorn, was galloping super fast around the frosty garden.

Crystal, Rosa's unicorn, was making a snow twister dance across the lawn, and Whisper, Ariana's unicorn, was standing under a tree with a family of timid rabbits playing around his hooves.

When the young unicorns and students first arrived at Unicorn Academy, they were put into pairs by the head teacher, Ms. Nettles. The students lived at the academy and attended classes, where they were taught how to care for their unicorns and learned all about their home on beautiful Unicorn Island. They also had to discover their unicorn's magic power and bond with them. While most unicorns and riders could bond in a year, some needed to stay for an extra year.

Violet's hands played with Twinkle's thick blue-and-purple mane. When they finally bonded, a strand of her dark hair would turn the same colors. She bent down and hugged him. "I hope we find your magic soon," she whispered. Violet loved being at the academy, but she didn't want to be the only one of her friends who stayed for another year.

"Don't worry," Twinkle said confidently. "We will. I bet I'll have something much better than Whisper's or Crystal's magic."

"Shh!" Violet hushed him as her friends came riding over.

"I don't know about all of you, but I'm ready for hot chocolate," said Rosa.

"Me too, and the unicorns deserve lots of sky berries," said Matilda.

The unicorns whickered happily. Doing magic used a lot of energy, and sky berries were really good for helping them recover.

Diamond dorm rode across the grounds. It was a frosty winter's day, and the school buildings were framed by the blue sky, the glass-and-marble towers sparkling in the pale sunlight.

"It's so strange to think we won't be here after graduation at the end of December," said Ariana.

"Twinkle and I might still be," said Violet. She

gave her friends a worried look. "You'll all write to me, won't you?"

"No," said Rosa.

Violet's heart sank.

Rosa grinned. "We're not going to write because you're not going to be here. You and Twinkle will discover his magic and bond very soon. We're all going to graduate together. It'll be perfect!"

The others smiled, and Violet felt a little better.

"It would be even more perfect if we could catch the cloaked figure before we graduate," said Freya.

During their year at the academy, the girls in Diamond dorm had come across a mysterious cloaked woman three times. Back in the spring, they had found out that she was taking magic from the Verdant Falls. And in the summer, they had discovered she was draining magic from the ancient Heart Tree. A month ago, she had tried

to scare them out of a barn on the school grounds where they had been planning a secret party. It turned out that the barn hid the entrance to a bunch of hidden tunnels. The mysterious woman had been using the tunnels to move around the school unseen, but no one knew why.

"I'm glad the teachers put protection spells on all the entrances to the tunnels so that only teachers and students can use them now," said Violet. Knowing that had made her feel much safer.

"I just wish we could work out who the cloaked figure is," said Freya.

"We've got lots of clues." Rosa started counting them off on her fingers. "One, she's been gathering magic power. Two, she knows a great deal about the school and its hidden tunnels. Three, her unicorn is tall and fast, has a long golden mane, and can cast glamours."

"And four, she wears shoes with a diamond pattern on the soles," added Violet, remembering some footprints they had found when exploring the tunnels.

"Could it be Ms. Bramble?" asked Matilda. "Her knife was found beside the Heart Tree when its magic was being drained. She told us she didn't know how it got there, but she could have been lying."

"Ms. Bramble might be grumpy, but she really seems to care about the island. I can't imagine her doing anything bad," said Ariana.

"And she doesn't have a unicorn that looks like the cloaked figure's unicorn," Freya pointed out. "None of the teachers do."

"So it can't be a teacher," said Violet, feeling relieved. She hated the thought of any of the academy teachers being evil.

"Whoever the cloaked figure is, I bet we haven't

seen the last of her," said Rosa. "We must keep our eyes and ears open. Agreed?"

"Agreed!" they all said together.

At the stables, they were dismounting when Ms. Willow, the school nurse, came walking across the grass from the school. She was young and friendly, and the girls really liked her.

"Did you have a nice ride?" she said, smiling.

"A frosty one!" said Violet, her breath coming out in little white puffs.

"Well, don't hang around here too long. You don't want to catch colds." Ms. Willow smiled. "Though if you do, I've just brewed a big bottle of special cold-cure medicine, so come and see me! Now it's time for Daffodil to have some of her health tonic, and I've got some lovely new ribbons for her mane." Ms. Willow loved her unicorn, Daffodil, and was always pampering her.

Diamond dorm took their unicorns inside and

started making sure they had thick, warm beds of straw to lie on and bulging hay nets to eat.

As Violet fetched Twinkle some sky berries, she caught sight of Ms. Willow braiding Daffodil's yellow-and-orange mane. The little unicorn's eyes were half closed. Violet felt a pang of envy. She wished Twinkle would let her take care of him like that, but he didn't like being brushed or having his mane played with. As Ms. Willow turned away to get some scissors, Daffodil lifted her head and looked at Violet. It was a strange look, almost like she wanted to tell her something. Ms. Willow turned back. Seeing Daffodil staring, she glanced around and caught sight of Violet. "Can I help you, dear?"

Violet blushed. "I was just getting some sky berries," she muttered. She left quickly, but the odd expression in Daffodil's eyes stayed with her as she filled Twinkle's bucket in the feed room.

She glanced back. Ms. Willow was now feeding Daffodil a tonic and murmuring in her ear. Daffodil's eyes were half shut again. Violet shook her head. She must have imagined the strange look. She headed back to Twinkle's stall.

"Sky berries!" Twinkle whinnied in delight, plunging his head into the bucket.

"Wait a moment, greedy guts!" Violet laughed. "Let me put them in the manger first."

She emptied the berries into the manger, and he started to gobble them up. "Yum! Thank you!"

Violet stepped closer, wondering if she dared to put an arm around his neck and cuddle him, when he raised his head.

"Listen, Violet," he said, through a mouthful of berries. "We really need to find my magic and bond as soon as possible. I think we should spend more time together."

Violet's heart lifted. "Yes, I could come to the stables more and brush you and braid ribbons in your mane and—"

"Boring!" Twinkle snorted. "No, I was thinking we could go on some nighttime rides, galloping under the stars. Just you and me." He looked eagerly at her. "It's a great idea, isn't it?"

He looked so pleased with himself that Violet didn't have the heart to tell him that she would really rather spend time in the stables, cuddling him and talking. She nodded. "Okay, let's do it."

"I knew you'd love my idea," Twinkle said

happily. "I'm sure it'll help us bond. Shall we go tonight?"

"I can't. There's an inter-dorm quiz tonight," said Violet. "But we could go tomorrow."

"Tomorrow it is, then!" Twinkle gave her a quick nuzzle before plunging his nose into the manger again.

Violet sighed. She loved that Twinkle was full of ideas, but sometimes she wished he would listen to what she wanted to do. Still, maybe going on nighttime rides really would help them bond. *Oh, I hope so,* Violet thought. *I really want to be able to graduate with our friends!*

CHAPTER 2

The quiz was fun but very competitive. At the last question, Diamond and Ruby dorms were tied for the lead. Ms. Rosemary, the Care of Unicorns teacher, smiled at the sea of faces as she asked, "Which bird has yellow, orange, and red feathers?" Isla from Ruby dorm stuck her hand in the air. "Isla?"

"The sun carrot!" shouted Isla. "Noooooo! I mean the sun—"

"Wrong!" said Ms. Rosemary, barely making her voice heard over everyone's laughter. "Sorry, Isla, I have to take your first answer. Anyone else?"

"The sun parrot," said Matilda. "Yay! Diamond girls win!" She fell on her friends, pulling them in for a group hug. But when Ms. Rosemary gave Diamond dorm their prize—a huge bag of candy—Matilda shared it with the girls from Ruby dorm, saying, "Because Isla helped us win and made us laugh."

Munching her candy and looking around at all the laughing students, Violet felt a tingly rush of happiness. She was so lucky to be at Unicorn Academy. If she could just bond with Twinkle and find his magic, everything really would be perfect!

The following morning, everyone crowded into the stables for a lesson on bonding, taught by Ms. Rosemary. It was a cold day, and Violet was thankful for her thick woolly socks and snuggly blue Unicorn Academy hoodie. She listened

eagerly to Ms. Rosemary, wanting to learn all she could.

"Any questions?" Ms. Rosemary finally asked when she'd finished her talk.

Violet hesitated. She had something to ask, but what if her question was silly? She started to raise her hand, but then changed her mind. However, Ms. Rosemary noticed.

"Violet, you look like you have a question," she said with a smile. "Don't worry. You can ask anything."

"Er, I just wondered if there's ever been a rider and unicorn who haven't bonded?" Violet's face warmed as everyone looked at her.

"Well, that's so rare it almost never happens. Riders and their unicorns nearly always bond within two years."

Violet felt relieved.

Isla put up her hand. "Can someone force a

unicorn to bond with them? Last year, a unicorn was stolen from near my home. My mom said she didn't understand why someone would do that because no unicorn would work with someone else when they'd already bonded. But what if the stolen unicorn was forced to bond again?"

"That would be awful!" said Matilda, stroking Pearl's nose.

"I couldn't bear it," said Rosa, hugging Crystal.

"I've never heard of any unicorn being stolen," said Valentina, who was also from Ruby dorm. She rolled her eyes. "I bet it's just a rumor that someone started to scare people."

"Actually, Valentina, it's not a rumor—it's true," said Ms. Rosemary. "It was a unicorn named Prancer, and what happened was terrible." She shook her head. "I knew Prancer well. I was friends with her partner, Lacey, when we were students here at the academy. Prancer was a splendid

unicorn with the longest mane I've ever seen. It was pure gold. She was also a very powerful spell weaver—a unicorn who can put their magic into any spell."

"She can't have been very powerful if she allowed herself to be stolen," said Twinkle, with an unimpressed snort. "No one could steal me away from Violet. I wouldn't let them."

Violet blushed at his rudeness.

"Well, I'm sure you'd put up a good fight, Twinkle," said Ms. Rosemary kindly. "But if a unicorn as powerful as Prancer was taken, then no unicorn is safe. However, here at Unicorn Academy, you will be fine, so please don't worry. And, in answer to your original question, Isla— no, no one can force a unicorn to bond with them. It simply isn't possible. A unicorn might be forced to work for someone through dark magic, but not to bond. Bonding only happens when the time is right and a rider and their unicorn become true friends." Ms. Rosemary beamed at the class. "Let's end here and go out for a ride!"

"That was a really interesting lesson," Violet said to Freya as they headed to their unicorns' stalls.

"Hmm?" Freya looked miles away.

"What's up?" asked Violet.

"It's just the name of that unicorn who was stolen—Prancer—I'm sure I've heard it before," said Freya.

"Me too!" exclaimed Matilda, overhearing.

"I haven't," said Violet, puzzled.

"So where did we hear it?" said Freya, frowning at Matilda.

Matilda shrugged. "I don't know."

"I thought Ms. Rosemary would never stop talking," said Twinkle to Violet when she went into his stall. "She went on and on, didn't she?"

Violet had enjoyed the lesson, but she didn't want to disagree with him. "I guess she did."

"It'll be fun going out now with everyone, but we are still going for a ride on our own tonight, aren't we?" Twinkle nudged her with his nose.

Violet nodded. "I'll come here right after dinner."

Twinkle snorted happily. "Yay! I can't wait!"

All day, Violet kept thinking about everything Ms. Rosemary had told them. Bonding happened when a rider and their unicorn became true friends, so why hadn't she and Twinkle bonded yet? She was sure they were already true friends. They loved each other and never argued—she always just let him have his way. It didn't make sense.

"Is anyone up for a game of Hungry Unicorns?" Ariana asked before dinner. Everyone said yes, and Ariana went to the cupboard to get the board game. But as she opened the door, a pile of drawings fell out. "Matilda!" she said impatiently. "Are these yours?"

"Yep. Sorry. I threw them in there the other day when we had to clean the dorm, then forgot about them," said Matilda, who loved to draw and paint.

"What a surprise!" Ariana rolled her eyes. She

was super neat and clean, and Matilda's messiness annoyed her. She helped Matilda gather up the drawings.

Suddenly Matilda stopped, her mouth falling open as she held up a sketch. "Prancer! I *thought* I knew the name!" She swung around to Freya. "There's a picture of a unicorn called Prancer hanging in the secret tower room above our dorm. I copied it when we were up there working on your unicorn robot!"

"Let me see." Rosa took the paper from Matilda as everyone gathered around. It was a drawing of a magnificent unicorn with a long golden mane.

"Do you think it's the same Prancer who was stolen?" asked Freya.

"It could be," said Ariana. "It looks just like the unicorn Ms. Rosemary described."

"Let's go see the picture," said Rosa.

Everyone rushed for the door, with Rosa leading the way up the spiral staircase, past their dorm and all the way to the secret room. They hadn't been there since the party a month ago.

Reaching the floor with the huge cupboard, Rosa looked at Freya. "It's really your room, Freya. You discovered it, so you open the door."

Hidden on the back wall of the cupboard was a lever. Freya pulled it, and with a muffled creak, the whole wall spun around. Violet and the others followed Freya through the cupboard and into the secret room behind it.

Shelves lined the curved walls and there was a large desk on one side, but the girls headed for a painting hanging on the wall over the fireplace. It was a picture of a tall unicorn with a flowing golden mane. The name *Prancer* was written beneath it.

Matilda gasped. "You know something? She looks just like the unicorn the cloaked figure rides. Do you think the unicorn was stolen?"

Freya nodded. "The cloaked figure's unicorn can gallop fast, appear and disappear, and cast glamours—all things a spell weaver can do."

PRANCER

Rosa paced around the tower room. "I wonder why there's a picture of her in here."

"Maybe the cloaked figure put it in this room for some reason?" Matilda said. "She tried to scare Freya and me away from here when we were working on the robot. Maybe she did that because there was something she wanted to use the room for."

"I bet you're right, Matilda!" Freya said. "And you know what? I think she's been in here since I last visited! Those jars of herbs on the shelves were full before, but now they're almost empty. And those are new." Freya marched over to the desk and pointed to some wiggly black marks scorched into the surface. "There was only one scorch mark before. I'm sure of it."

Ariana squeaked. "And look at that, everyone!" She pointed to a faint, diamond-patterned

footprint in the dust by the fireplace. "It's the same as the footprints we found in the tunnels!"

"The cloaked figure must have been using this room," said Rosa in excitement.

"Wait!" Violet didn't like disagreeing with her friends, but she'd had an important thought. "What about the spells the teachers put on the entrances to the tunnels? The cloaked figure shouldn't be able to use them to come up here anymore."

There was a moment of silence as they all thought about it.

"True—" Freya began.

"Unless," interrupted Rosa, "the cloaked figure is someone who's part of the school, so the spells don't work on her!"

"A teacher?" breathed Matilda.

"But we've already said none of the teachers' unicorns look like Prancer," Violet pointed out.

"So maybe it's a student?" Freya gasped. "Some of the students' unicorns have golden manes. I know Valentina's unicorn, Golden Briar, does."

"I don't know," said Rosa. "But I think we need to do some serious investigating."

"I think what we need to do is tell Ms. Nettles what we've found," said Ariana.

"Me too," said Violet.

"Not yet," said Rosa quickly. "I think we should wait and see if we can find out anything more."

"I'm with Rosa," said Matilda, her eyes shining. "Let's try to solve the mystery ourselves. Freya, you agree with us, don't you?"

Freya hesitated, but then nodded. "I guess so. If we all stick together, we should be safe. We may be able to find out more than the teachers,

because the cloaked figure won't be expecting us to be looking for her."

"It'll be fun," Rosa declared. "Come on, Violet. You know you want to solve the mystery!"

Ariana glanced at Violet as if to say, *If you don't give in, then I won't, either.* Violet felt torn. She wanted to tell Ms. Nettles, but she didn't want to upset the others. Sending Ariana an apologetic smile, Violet gave in.

"Okay," she said.

"Yay!" Rosa grinned at Ariana. "That's four against one."

Ariana sighed. "All right, we don't tell Ms. Nettles yet. But we have to be really careful."

"We will be!" Rosa promised her.

As they all fist-bumped, the pencil that Matilda usually carried behind her ear fell to the ground and rolled under the desk. Crouching down to pick it up, she frowned. "What's this?" She

held up a scrap of silvery-gray fabric with burnt edges.

"It looks like an old piece of material," said Freya.

"It might be a clue," said Violet, looking over Freya's shoulder. The fabric was shimmery and very soft.

The sound of a bell ringing in the distance made them all jump.

"It's dinnertime," said Ariana. "We'd better go downstairs."

Rosa grinned. "Then after dinner we can think of a plan. We're going to solve this mystery— I just know we are!"

CHAPTER 3

"Planning time!" announced Rosa happily when they all gathered in Diamond dorm after dinner.

Violet really wanted to stay, but she had to keep her promise to Twinkle. "I'm sorry, but I've got to go to the stables."

"Why?" Matilda asked.

"Twinkle wants us to spend time together—he thinks it might help us bond," she explained.

Her friends nodded. "Then you should go," said Freya.

"Definitely," said Matilda.

Violet put on her coat and gloves and slipped out

of the dorm. It was very cold outside. Her feet crunched on the frosty grass. Glancing up at the sky, she hoped it wouldn't snow.

There was a rustle in some nearby bushes. A shiver ran down her spine. What if the cloaked figure was also out in the garden? Feeling uneasy, she sprinted to the stables. It was a relief to dive inside. As she breathed in the sweet smell of hay and let her heart slow down, she heard a murmur of voices from Twinkle's stall. Who was he talking to? Violet went closer and listened.

"Try not to worry about it," Daffodil was saying in a kind voice. "You will find your magic soon and bond with Violet, I know it."

Violet smiled at Daffodil's words of encouragement. The little unicorn was as kind as Ms. Willow.

"It's hard not to worry," Twinkle admitted. "I don't want to let Violet down, Daffodil."

Violet felt a rush of surprise. She didn't know Twinkle worried about things like that.

"You won't let her down," said Daffodil. "You'll bond soon, and then you'll be together forever."

Violet caught a note of wistfulness in her voice, but Twinkle didn't seem to notice.

"I wish I could do something to make it happen."

"This starlight ride is an excellent idea. The more time you spend together the better," said Daffodil. "Have fun. You only get one special partner, Twinkle. Make the most of it." She left his stall and went slowly back to her own. Violet watched her with a frown. Daffodil looked upset. But why?

She waited until Daffodil went into her stall before she stepped out of the shadows, pretending that she'd just arrived. "Hi, Twinkle. What's going on?"

"Nothing much," said Twinkle quickly.

Violet wondered why he didn't mention his talk with Daffodil.

"Let's get going," he said. "It's a cold night. It might even snow!"

They left the stables and rode over to the stream at the bottom of the meadow, where they stopped and watched the dark water flow by.

The starlight made the water glitter. In a nearby

tree, an owl hooted softly. Twinkle sighed happily. "I love nighttime, when the stars are shining," he said. "It makes me feel all tingly. Do you like it too?"

"Oh yes," agreed Violet.

It was lovely being there with Twinkle, but she could feel the cold seeping in despite her thick gloves and socks. She also kept thinking about his conversation with Daffodil. Why hadn't he mentioned it?

"Twinkle . . ."

"You're shivering!"

They had spoken at the same time.

"You first," said Violet.

"I can feel that you're cold," he said, sounding worried. "Put your hands in my mane to warm them up."

Violet sank her hands into Twinkle's long mane and immediately felt warmer, both inside and

out. "That's better," she said, gazing up at the sparkling sky.

"Look, a shooting star!" said Twinkle. "Make a wish, Violet!"

They both watched the star arcing over them.

"Do you think we wished the same thing?" Twinkle asked.

Violet smiled. "I think we might have."

"Now, what were you going to say?" asked Twinkle.

Violet had wanted to ask about Daffodil's visit, but she didn't feel like ruining the moment. "It was nothing important. This is so nice—just being here with you. The two of us together."

Twinkle stamped a hoof. "It really is, but even I'm getting cold now."

A pink spark caught Violet's eye. Had that just flown up from Twinkle's hoof? Hope bubbled inside her as she breathed in a faint scent of burnt

sugar—the smell of magic. "Twinkle, did you see that?"

"See what?" he asked.

Violet hesitated. The spark had vanished, and she didn't want to get his hopes up just in case she'd imagined it. "Nothing. Should we walk on a little way and try to warm up?"

"Cantering will do that better than walking!" said Twinkle.

They cantered off, leaving the meadow behind them and entering the trees beyond it. A chilly wind picked up, and Violet pulled her hood over her head, grateful for its softness and warmth. She stroked Twinkle's neck and let him pick his way through the trees, slowing to watch a family of storm raccoons playing in a clearing. Violet was enjoying herself so much that she hardly noticed the first few flakes of snow. It was only when they came out of the trees that she realized

it was snowing heavily. "It's a blizzard, Twinkle!" Snow was falling so thickly, she couldn't even see the school.

"Should we go back?" Twinkle asked.

Violet shivered as the flakes landed on her coat. "I think we'd better."

Twinkle set off into the snowstorm. The flakes covered them both with a cold white layer. Worry swirled through Violet. What if they got lost? What if they froze? She squeaked, her hands clutching at Twinkle's neck as he stumbled over a stone.

"Don't worry, Violet. We're going to be fine. I'll look after you, I promise," said

Twinkle, stamping his feet as he marched through the snow.

Violet felt her panic start to fade. Nothing bad was going to happen, not when Twinkle was with her. She sat up a bit taller and blinked. Weird. It was still snowing, but the snow wasn't landing on them anymore. It was almost like they had a huge umbrella protecting them. Violet caught a whiff of burnt sugar, and Twinkle gave a surprised snort. "What's going on?" she said. "Twinkle—"

She broke off as a flurry of snowflakes landed on her head, making her gasp out loud. She must have imagined it. Snowflakes were certainly landing on her now! But, she realized, she could see the lights of the school ahead. "We're almost back, Twinkle!" she said.

"I'll have us home safe and sound in no time at all," he said, breaking into a canter.

"Where are you going? This isn't the way to the stables," Violet said as Twinkle turned away from the stables and headed toward the school.

"I'm going to take you back first." Twinkle cantered up to the academy and stopped at the door. "You go in and get warm."

"No," said Violet, through chattering teeth. "Take me back to the stables so I can brush the snow from your coat. You'll catch a cold if you sleep when you're wet."

Twinkle chuckled. "I'll be fine. I'll roll in my straw bed to get dry. Now stop arguing or I'll carry you all the way up to your dorm!"

"Twinkle!" Violet groaned, but she had to admit that she didn't mind him looking after her. "Are you sure?"

"Absolutely," he said. "You mean everything to me, Violet. Keeping you safe is the most important thing in the world."

"Really?" Violet slid from his back and threw her arms around him.

Twinkle let her hug him for once. "Yes, really," he said, nuzzling her. "Now go!"

"But how will I know you get back safely?" she asked. "That's just as important to me."

"Watch me from inside. And don't worry, I'll be back in my warm stall in two shakes of a unicorn's tail."

Violet kissed him. "All right. Night, Twinkle."

She ran inside and watched from a window as he cantered back to the stables. The starlight ride had been much more adventurous than she had expected! Suddenly she remembered the pink spark she'd seen when they'd been standing in the meadow, looking at the stars—she was sure she had seen it. Had that been a hint that Twinkle's magic was going to appear soon? Feeling a flutter of excitement and hope, she ran upstairs to the dorm.

CHAPTER 4

Violet's friends were all very relieved to see her. "We've been worried about you," said Ariana, hurrying over. "We thought you might be lost in the snow."

"We were, but Twinkle was amazing." Violet sat on her bed and pulled her thick blanket around her. She told the others how Twinkle had brought them safely back through the snow. She decided not to tell them about the pink spark, just in case she'd imagined it.

Matilda hugged her. "Well, I'm glad you're back."

Violet smiled. Her friends were the best!

"Do you want to hear what we've decided to do about the cloaked figure?" said Rosa, her eyes shining. She jumped onto Violet's bed. "Tomorrow night, we're going to sneak into the teachers' rooms and spy on them!"

Matilda grinned, but Freya frowned. "I really don't think it's a good idea."

"Freya and Ariana have said they won't come, but you will, won't you, Violet?" said Rosa.

"Um . . ."

"Pleeeeeeease!" said Matilda.

Violet really didn't want to. "Well . . ."

"We won't take no for an answer," said Rosa firmly.

"Oh, all right," said Violet. Rosa and Matilda beamed.

"Awesome! Tomorrow night, our spying mission begins!" Rosa said.

Violet was tired the next day. Ms. Bramble scolded Violet twice for yawning during her lesson on healing with herbs. Violet was extremely relieved when Ms. Bramble ended the lesson early and sent them to get lunch. After a warming bowl of soup with hot crusty bread, Violet and her friends went to the stables to visit their unicorns. Shouts of laughter greeted them across the yard. They hurried inside and found Miki, Himmat, and the other boys from Topaz dorm pretending to duel with hockey sticks.

"What's going on?" asked Rosa.

"Jake's fighting us! We tricked him. He's never played unicorn hockey before, so we told him the sticks were used to pull riders from their unicorns." Miki could hardly speak through his laughter.

Himmat doubled over. "And we told him once

you'd caught a rider, you used the stick to hook
him by his hoodie."

"I knew you were joking," said Jake, waving his
hockey stick.

"Did not!" yelled Miki and Himmat.

Rosa burst out laughing too. "That's mean.
Genius, but still mean!"

"We know!"

When everyone eventually calmed down, Freya

said, "Honey loves unicorn hockey. Who's up for a game in the snow, Diamond dorm against Topaz?"

"I'm in," said Ariana. "I'm terrible at hockey, but Whisper loves playing sports."

Twinkle looked out of his stall. "Hockey's boring," he said loudly.

Violet winced at his rudeness, but Himmat just grinned. "Oh, hockey's boring, is it? Obviously you've never played with us. Am I right, Miki?"

"Yeah," said Miki. "No one gets bored the way we play! Come on, Violet. You'll join, won't you?" He went to hand Violet a hockey stick, but Twinkle stepped out of the stall and stood in his way.

"Violet doesn't want to play hockey."

"Wow, Violet! You said that without even moving your mouth," joked Miki. He wiggled

a hockey stick at her, trying to pass it around Twinkle. "Go on, give it a try!"

"I . . . um . . . well . . ." Violet's cheeks burned as everyone turned to look at her. She really wanted to play, but she didn't want to disagree with Twinkle, especially after their closeness last night.

"Violet?" said Himmat.

Violet didn't know what to do. "Sorry," she gasped suddenly. "I've got a headache. I'm going back to the dorm." She hurried away, sure that everyone would guess she was chickening out. Why couldn't Twinkle just ask what she wanted to do for a change? Once she was outside the stables, she ran all the way to the academy. She yanked the door open and almost bumped into Isla, who was on her way out.

"Whoops! Sorry!" said Isla. She frowned. "Hey, are you okay, Violet?"

47

"I'm fine," muttered Violet.

Isla looked doubtful. "You don't look fine." She pulled Violet inside and over to a large window seat. "What's up?"

Violet found herself blurting out what had happened, and once she'd started, she couldn't stop. Soon Isla knew all her concerns about Twinkle. "I don't think he means to be rude," Violet finished. "But I can't help thinking that we'll never bond if he doesn't listen to me or think about what I want."

Isla gave Violet's arm a squeeze. "Twinkle hasn't always been this rude, has he?" she asked. "He's the last unicorn in your dorm who hasn't found his magic or bonded. I bet he's worried, and that's why he's bossier than normal. Maybe you should try talking to him about what you want when he starts making decisions for both of you."

Violet squirmed. "He'll get upset. I'd rather just not say anything and make him happy."

"But that isn't making *you* happy," Isla pointed out.

Violet swallowed and voiced her biggest fear. "Oh, Isla, what if we don't ever bond?"

"Of course you will! I haven't bonded with Buttercup yet, either, but it'll happen. Remember what Ms. Rosemary said in the lesson? It's very rare for a rider and their unicorn not to bond." Isla took Violet's hand. "We've got to keep believing that."

Violet nodded, and the two girls shared a hopeful smile.

CHAPTER 5

To Violet's relief, when everyone returned from unicorn hockey, rosy-cheeked and chatting happily, they didn't mention what happened in the stables with Twinkle. "So, tonight!" Rosa said, bouncing up to Violet. "We'll start snooping after dinner. Okay?"

"Okay," said Violet reluctantly.

"You don't have to go, Violet," said Ariana. "You can stay with Freya and me."

"Nope, Violet's coming with us," said Rosa. "And that's that!"

Before bedtime, Violet found herself shivering in

a dark hall in the teachers' building as she crept behind Rosa and Matilda. Every cell in her body was wishing she was back in Diamond dorm with Freya and Ariana.

"What exactly are we looking for, Rosa?" asked Matilda. She swung her flashlight wildly, sending a dancing beam of light along the ceiling.

"Shoes!" announced Rosa. "We're going to see if any of the teachers' shoes have a diamond pattern on the sole."

Violet really didn't want to sneak into the teachers' rooms. "How about we look in the staff cloakroom?" she suggested.

Rosa's eyes sparkled. "Ooh, yes! Good plan. The teachers will all be in their common room after dinner."

The staff cloakroom was near the back door. It was lined with shoe racks underneath. "Look at all these shoes," Matilda whispered as they went

inside and shut the door behind them. "It's going to take ages to check them."

The girls set to work, using their flashlights to see the soles of the riding boots and shoes. Rosa and Matilda were soon giggling.

"Look at this!" said Matilda, pulling a pink, yellow, and very fluffy sock out of a boot and carefully holding it up. "Whose is it?"

"Ms. Bramble's?" Rosa said innocently, causing Matilda to snort loudly.

Matilda dropped the sock back into the boot and then pulled out a pair of old green socks from another pair of shoes. "Eew! Smelly!" she squealed, dropping them. She and Rosa rocked with laughter.

Violet's heart was thumping, and it beat even faster when she heard a creak outside. "Shhh," she said. "What's that?"

But Rosa and Matilda were giggling too hard and didn't hear her.

"Quiet!" Violet hissed.

The door opened and the light snapped on. Matilda squeaked, and Violet's flashlight clattered to the floor.

"Girls!" Ms. Willow stood in the doorway, dressed in a thick scarf and outdoor coat and holding an empty bottle of Daffodil's tonic. "What are you doing in here?"

Violet felt like crying. They were going to

get into so much trouble. She'd known this was a bad idea.

"We . . . um . . ." For once even Rosa didn't know what to say.

Ms. Willow looked at them for a moment, and then her lips twitched into a  smile. "Hmm. Now, let me see. Were you trying to find me, maybe? Because you were feeling ill?"

Violet blinked. It sounded almost like Ms. Willow was trying to give them a way out—an excuse for being there.

"Yes," said Matilda, her eyes widening. "We felt unwell."

Rosa nodded. "We thought . . . We thought we might be getting sick."

"Well, in that case, I'll overlook you all being here, as long as it doesn't happen again. Now, why don't you hurry along to bed, and I'll bring you some of my cold-cure medicine. Unless you're already feeling a bit better?" Ms. Willow's eyes twinkled.

"Actually, I think we'll be fine," Rosa said.

Violet couldn't believe it. Thank goodness lovely Ms. Willow had found them! If Ms. Brambles or Ms. Rivers had discovered them, they would certainly have been sent straight to Ms. Nettles.

Ms. Willow followed the girls out of the cloakroom. "Go back to your dorm, girls. If I hear any noise, I'll be up with that cold-cure medicine in a stamp of a unicorn's hoof. Understand?"

"We understand!" they all answered as they scurried away.

"Phew! That was close!" said Rosa, when they'd turned a corner.

Matilda blew out a long breath. "Hooray for Ms. Willow!"

Violet nodded, feeling upset with herself. She'd known all along that Rosa's spying mission was a bad idea. So why had she gone along with it? *If anyone asks me again to do something I don't want to do, I'm definitely going to say no*, she decided, *even if it's Twinkle!* But would she really argue with him? Not wanting to think about it, Violet squashed her thoughts down and quickly ran upstairs with the others.

CHAPTER 6

"Get up, sleepy." Violet woke to find Ariana gently shaking her.

Violet sat up slowly, blinking the sleep from her eyes. Hot shame flooded through her as she remembered the spying and being caught by Ms. Willow. She glanced over at Rosa and Matilda. Neither of them seemed bothered. In fact, Rosa was gleefully reenacting the moment in the cloakroom when they'd been caught.

"It was so funny," she said to the others. "You should have seen our faces!"

"Lucky it was only Ms. Willow," said Freya.

Rosa nodded. "She's the best. Well, I guess that means we can't do any more nighttime spying."

"Good," said Ariana. "Does that mean we can tell Ms. Nettles?"

"Just a few more days," begged Rosa. "And if we haven't found anything else by then, we can tell her. I promise!"

At lunchtime, Violet slipped away from her friends and went to the stables to see Twinkle. He was talking to Daffodil and looked surprised to see her.

"Do we have a lesson now?" he asked. "I thought it was lunchtime."

"It is," said Violet. "I just thought I'd spend some time with you. I could braid some ribbons into your mane? Daffodil's ribbons look really pretty."

A strange expression crossed Daffodil's face

but was gone so quickly Violet must have imagined it.

"Twinkle was just telling me about your adventure the other night," said Daffodil. "It sounds very exciting."

Twinkle snorted. "It was! Why don't we go out for a ride now, Violet? The snow's gone."

Violet took a breath and lifted her chin. "I want to stay in and braid your mane."

Twinkle looked surprised. "But I want to go out."

"Twinkle, maybe you should do what Violet wants to do for a change," suggested Daffodil. "You always seem to make the decisions for the pair of you."

"Do I?" Twinkle blinked. "Oh, all right, we can stay in and you can put ribbons in my mane, Violet."

Violet blinked. She'd gotten what she wanted without an argument! "Great!" she said, hardly believing it. "I'll go get some!"

"Daffodil!" Violet heard Ms. Willow singing Daffodil's name as she came into the stables. "Where are you, my sweetie? Come here!"

Daffodil tensed. "I've got to go."

Violet skipped to the storeroom and chose some red and gold ribbons. As she returned to Twinkle's stall, she saw Ms. Willow stroking Daffodil.

"Hello, Violet." To Violet's relief, Ms. Willow greeted her as if nothing had happened the night before. "How are you today? Are you feeling better?" Her eyes twinkled.

"Yes, thank you," said Violet, blushing. She looked at the ribbon Ms. Willow had in her hands. "That's a nice ribbon," she said, changing the subject. The ribbon was very unusual. It had a pearly sheen that was almost silver. It reminded Violet of something, but she couldn't remember what.

"I like Daffodil to look pretty," said Ms. Willow. "Time for your tonic, Daffodil, and then I'll get braiding."

Violet returned to Twinkle's stall. But as she reached it, she stopped. An image of the fabric that Matilda had found in the secret room flashed into her head. The ribbon Ms. Willow had been holding was the same silvery color. Frowning, Violet went back to Daffodil's stall.

Ms. Willow was just putting the tonic bottle down. She glanced around and asked, "Is everything all right, dear? You look worried."

"Yes, I just, er . . . I really like that ribbon you have. Where did you get it?"

"Just from the storeroom." Ms. Willow held the ribbon up. "It's a lovely shade of purple, isn't it?"

Violet blinked. Purple? She'd been sure the ribbon was silver. But, no, the ribbon Ms. Willow was holding was definitely a deep purple. Her eyes must be playing tricks on her.

"I'm sure you'll find some in the storeroom if you look," said Ms. Willow, smiling.

"Thanks. I'll go look later," said Violet. Feeling a bit silly, she turned away.

"Matilda, do you have that piece of material we found in the secret room?" Violet asked later as she got ready for afternoon lessons.

"Sure, it's somewhere around here." Matilda started to hunt around her bed, opening drawers. "Now, where did I put it?"

"You put it in here when we came down from the secret room," said Ariana, opening Matilda's jewelry box.

"Oh yes!" said Matilda. "Thanks." She handed it to Violet. "What do you want it for?"

"I just want to look at it." Violet turned the material from side to side. It had the same silvery gleam as the ribbon that she was sure she had seen Ms. Willow holding. *Why did I think Ms. Willow's ribbon looked like*

this? Violet wondered. *Were my eyes playing tricks on me?*

"Are you okay?" Ariana asked.

"Yeah." But Violet felt something nagging at her. It wasn't just the ribbon. Something else was bothering her. What was it? Turning the scrap of material over in her hands, she realized. Daffodil! When Ms. Willow had come into the stables, Daffodil had tensed up as though she was scared.

Violet almost laughed out loud. That was ridiculous! Everyone knew how much Ms. Willow cared for Daffodil. She had to be mistaken.

I'll talk to Twinkle, she decided. *He's friends with Daffodil—he might have noticed something.* She'd ask him if he wanted to go on another ride that night, and they could talk then. Happiness fizzed through her as she remembered how much fun they'd had on the first ride until it had started snowing. It would be lovely to be out with him again. Just the two of them, in the peace of a starlit night.

Violet had cross-country that afternoon and didn't have a chance to talk to Twinkle about going on a starlight ride until afterward. As she filled his hay net, Twinkle left his stall to talk to Daffodil. They were whispering about something when Ms. Willow came into the stable. Daffodil gave Twinkle a quick nuzzle. "We'll speak more later, Twinkle," Violet heard her say softly, before she trotted over to join Ms. Willow.

"What were you two talking about?" Violet asked curiously as she and Twinkle went back to his stall.

"Just this and that," he said, shrugging.

Violet frowned. It wasn't like Twinkle to hide things from her. "What sort of this and that?"

Twinkle looked awkward. "Just unicorn stuff. You . . . you wouldn't understand."

Violet felt a stab of hurt. Why would he think she wouldn't understand? And what could he possibly have been talking about that he couldn't share with her? For a moment, she almost felt like she didn't want to go for a ride that evening after all, but then she told herself not to be silly. She needed to talk to him in private.

"I was thinking," she said, pushing her hurt aside. "How about we go for another starlight ride tonight?" She expected him to nod eagerly, but, to her surprise, he looked worried.

"Tonight? No, I can't. Not tonight!"

Violet stared. "What? Why?"

"I . . . I don't want to. I'm . . . tired." He started

yawning widely. "Yes, I'm very, very tired."

Violet frowned. "Twinkle, you're not tired."

"I am," insisted Twinkle, avoiding her gaze. "I really am."

Violet didn't know what to do. He was obviously lying about feeling tired, but why? Feeling hurt, she tied up his hay net and picked up her coat. "Okay, well, I'll see you in the morning," she muttered.

"Wait, Violet!" A mix of emotions swirled in Twinkle's eyes. "I can't meet you tonight, but

come see me in the morning." He nodded. "Yes, in the morning, everything will be fine. Please come talk to me then."

"Okay," Violet said slowly. "I'll see you in the morning. Night, Twinkle." Frowning, she hurried away.

CHAPTER 7

On the way back to school, all Violet could think about was Twinkle. Why was he being so secretive? And what had he meant when he said everything would be fine by the morning? Something didn't feel right. It sounded like he was planning something—but what?

In the dining room, Diamond and Topaz dorms were sharing a table. Although dinner was her favorite, lasagna, Violet only picked at it. She couldn't leave things as they were with Twinkle. Even if it was hard, she had to go back and talk to him. Clearing away her half-empty plate, she

slipped out. She put on her coat and boots and ran across the frosty lawn in the dark. As she got close to the stables, Twinkle came out. Her heart stopped. Where was he going?

"Twinkle!" Her voice sounded loud in the quiet night.

He froze.

"What are you doing?" she asked.

Twinkle avoided her eyes. "Um . . . going out. For . . . for a walk."

"At this time?" Violet forgot about not arguing with him—she'd had enough. She marched in front of Twinkle. "Stop lying to me!" she told him hotly. Twinkle's gaze flew to her face as she put her hands on her hips. "I mean it, Twinkle. I'm standing here until you tell me what's going on!" She was shaking with emotion. She didn't usually get angry, but this was too important. She had to know what Twinkle was up to. She waited

70

for him to argue, but, to her surprise, he hung his head.

"I'm meeting Daffodil," he muttered.

"What? Why?" said Violet.

"She said she has something important to tell me, but she said we need to be outside in the starlight." Twinkle's dark eyes shone with excitement as he looked up. "Violet, I think it might be a way of speeding up the bonding process. Daffodil knows a lot about magic, and she knows how much I want to bond with you. I think she might be able to help me."

Violet frowned. "But, Twinkle, Ms. Rosemary said bonding happens when the time is right. If there was a way of speeding it up, then I'm sure she would have told us. There can't be anything Daffodil can do."

Twinkle looked stubborn. "But I think there is. Why else would she say she had something

important to talk to me about? I want to go meet her, Violet."

Violet hesitated. Something didn't feel right.

"Please let me go," he begged.

Violet didn't want to agree, but she also didn't want to upset him. "Okay," she said. "But I'm coming with you."

"You don't need to," Twinkle began. "It's really cold out tonight."

"I don't care," said Violet. She gave him a firm look. "Either we go to meet Daffodil together, or you don't go at all, even if it means I have to stay in the stables with you all night."

She blinked. For a moment, she'd sounded a bit like Rosa! But it seemed to work.

Twinkle nodded. "All right. Let's go together. I'd rather you came with me anyway, but we'd better hurry or we'll be late. Daffodil said to meet her at the edge of the woods."

Violet climbed onto his back, and they set off at a canter across the frosty lawn.

As they approached the woods, Violet saw a shadowy figure in a cloak moving across the grass ahead of them. She clutched Twinkle's mane and gasped. It was the hooded figure! But just then, the moon came out from behind a cloud and showed the person more clearly. Violet breathed a

sigh of relief. No, it wasn't. It was just Ms. Willow. "Did Daffodil tell you Ms. Willow would be here too?" she asked.

Twinkle slowed to a trot. A note of uncertainty crept into his voice as he replied, "No."

"Stop!" gasped Violet, suddenly spotting something on the ground. She stared in disbelief. A set of footprints tracked Ms. Willow's progress across the frosty grass. Each footprint had a diamond-shaped pattern. "Twinkle! The footprints! They're just like the ones we found in the cave and in the secret room." An icy fear gripped her as Twinkle snorted in alarm and a horrible thought struck her. Could Ms. Willow be the cloaked figure who had been draining magic from the island?

CHAPTER 8

"She's seen us!" Violet squeaked as Ms. Willow swung around.

For a moment, she hoped she was wrong, that Ms. Willow was really just the lovely teacher she had always thought her to be. But then a furious frown came over Ms. Willow's face, and Violet's heart sank into her boots.

"I knew something was going on!" Ms. Willow's voice snapped through the night air like an icicle cracking. "Trying to outsmart me!" She gave a shrill whistle and Daffodil emerged from the trees. The little unicorn moved slowly, almost as if she

was fighting against leaving the woods but had no choice.

"Daffodil? You should know better!" said Ms. Willow. Daffodil sent Twinkle and Violet a desperate look but began to trot toward Ms. Willow.

Violet didn't know what was going on, but she did know that she and Twinkle had to get help—and fast!

"Come on, Twinkle!" she gasped. "Let's get back to the school!"

Twinkle spun around and set off at a gallop just as Daffodil reached Ms. Willow. Violet clung to his mane, her thoughts swirling. How could the cloaked figure be lovely Ms. Willow? It just didn't seem possible. Something rushed past them, and suddenly Ms. Willow and Daffodil appeared out of nowhere, blocking their way. Twinkle had to swerve to avoid crashing into them.

"There's no escape for you two now!" Ms. Willow hissed. Her voice sounded harsh and bitter, nothing like her usual soft tone. Before Twinkle or Violet could do anything, she flicked her hand. There was a flash of green, and the world tilted as Violet and Twinkle spun through the air.

Everything blurred. Violet's hands numbed as she desperately hung on to Twinkle's neck. Then they were falling. Violet tensed, expecting the worst. Twinkle's hooves sank into the ground,

and he landed with a bounce as the world came back into focus.

Above them, the inky night sky glittered with thousands of stars. Their light was reflected by the thick ice of a huge frozen lake, and Violet realized that they were standing right at its edge. At the far side, a strip of land separated it from a huge black sea. Beneath the layer of ice, the water looked dark.

"Where are we?" said Twinkle.

"I think it's the Frozen Lagoon!" breathed Violet. "We learned about it from Ms. Rivers a month ago. It's bottomless, always frozen, and no one's ever been able to find it because magic keeps its location secret."

A thin mist swirled like ghosts above the dark ice. Beneath the ice, they could see water bubbling. Violet shivered—the mist smelled sickly

sweet, and there was something unnatural about the way it was moving.

"Why do you think Ms. Willow brought us here?" said Twinkle.

"I don't know," said Violet. "I can't believe she's the cloaked figure, Twinkle. She always seemed so nice."

"I can't believe that Daffodil has been helping her," said Twinkle, shaking his head in disbelief.

"I don't understand. Whenever we saw the cloaked figure with a unicorn, it didn't look anything like Daffodil," said Violet. "It was taller, with a long golden mane, just like Prancer, the stolen unicorn."

"Maybe Ms. Willow has two unicorns," suggested Twinkle.

It seemed like the only thing that made sense.

Violet looked around. "What are we going to do now?"

"Try to escape?" said Twinkle.

There was a flash of green, and Ms. Willow and Daffodil landed nearby.

Twinkle reared bravely, slashing the air with his forelegs. Then, wheeling around, he galloped away. Ms. Willow's laughter echoed after him.

"You can run, but there's no escape from me!"

Violet ducked as something whizzed over her head. A bolt of magic hit the rocks in front of them, and the rocks exploded into shards. Twinkle swerved, and the sour smell of bad magic filled Violet's nostrils.

"Don't try to get away—you'll only get hurt," Daffodil called anxiously.

Twinkle swung around. "Daffodil, why are you helping her? I thought you were my friend!"

Ms. Willow smirked. "Oh, dear sweet Daffodil

has no choice! Those ribbons—the ones you admired so much, Violet—contain a powerful binding spell, and while they are in her mane, Daffodil must obey my every command. For some reason, she thought that she could warn you tonight about what was going on, but she should have known better. I have made it so she can't speak of my plans. Even if she had met with you, she couldn't have told you anything."

Daffodil gave Twinkle a desperate look. "I thought I would find a way and . . ." She gasped and fell silent as Ms. Willow glared at her.

"Let us go!" Violet cried.

"What?" sneered Ms. Willow. "And have you return to school and tell everyone about me? I think not. You will stay here while I finish my plans to force every unicorn on Unicorn Island to do what I want. I have spent years preparing for this. I am not going to let one silly girl and her

unicorn, who hasn't even found his magic, stop
me." She dismounted. "Daffodil—lock them up!"

Daffodil slowly trotted over to Twinkle and
Violet and started to herd them toward a stone
hut.

"My friends will wonder where I am. They'll
try to find me!" Violet shouted.

Ms. Willow's eyes narrowed. "Hmm, you may be right. They are always sticking their noses in everything. I'll deal with them too."

Violet caught her breath. "What do you mean? What—"

Ms. Willow snapped her fingers, and the door to the hut flew open.

Twinkle swung around and charged at Daffodil, but Ms. Willow sent a bolt of green magic from her fingertips. It flew right at him and Violet, knocking Twinkle off his feet and sending them flying backward. As they tumbled into the hut, the heavy wooden door slammed shut and the bolts locked in place. They were trapped!

CHAPTER 9

Violet thumped her fists against the door while Twinkle hit it with his hooves, but it held firm. Eventually, they sank back, exhausted.

"What are we going to do?" Violet cried. "We've got to get out of here and warn the others. If Ms. Willow captures them, it'll be our fault." She threw her arms around his neck.

Twinkle nuzzled her. "I'm sorry, Violet. I got us into this mess. I shouldn't have been so stubborn about meeting Daffodil."

Violet shook her head. "I agreed to go with you. But I wonder why she asked you to meet

her. It sounds like she wouldn't have been able to tell you anything about Ms. Willow's plans anyway."

"I don't know," said Twinkle. "She just said she wanted to meet me somewhere outside in the starlight to tell me something important, but that doesn't matter now. We need to try to get out of here." He pawed at the earth with a front hoof. "Maybe we could dig our way out."

The sudden sound of voices and whinnies outside the hut made Violet shudder. "Twinkle, we're too late!" She gasped.

"Where are we? Why have you brought us here?" she heard Rosa shout angrily.

"Let us go!" exclaimed Matilda.

"So you can ruin my plans, you annoying girls? Never!" Ms. Willow sneered. "I warned you about snooping around the school at night. You should have stayed in your dorm!"

"We were looking for Violet. She's missing." Ariana sounded close to tears.

"I'm in here with Twinkle!" Violet yelled through the door.

"Violet!" yelled Freya. "Help me, everyone. Let's get her out!"

"CHARGE!" Rosa shouted.

Violet's heart leaped as she heard the thunder of hooves. Ms. Willow shrieked, and suddenly the bolts of the hut door grated and the door swung open. Violet could hardly believe her eyes. Rosa, Matilda, and Ariana, riding their unicorns, had cornered Ms. Willow at the edge of the Frozen Lagoon. Meanwhile, Freya and Honey had reached the hut and pulled the bolts back.

"We're free!" gasped Twinkle as he cantered through the door.

Violet saw Ms. Willow raise her hands. "Watch

86

out!" she cried, guessing what she was about to do.

Three fiery bolts of green magic shot at Pearl's, Crystal's, and Whisper's legs, sending them and the girls tumbling onto the ice. In the chaos of shouts and whinnies, Ms. Willow scrambled to her feet and sent another two bolts of magic toward Freya and Violet.

Honey used her superspeed to get Freya to safety. Violet smelled a faint scent of burnt sugar, but the next moment she felt Twinkle barreling into her, knocking her to the ground. The green bolts of magic flashed past her head, burning through the ends of his mane. They hit the back wall of the hut, exploding in sparks that stung like needles as they hit Violet's face. There was no time to waste. Leaping up, Violet threw herself onto Twinkle's back. Freya and Honey were already at

the lagoon, shimmying onto the ice to help the others get to their feet.

Twinkle raced to join them.

Ms. Willow threw more firebolts at the girls and their unicorns. Hissing and spitting, the magical bolts cut through the ice, making it melt all around them.

"We're going to fall in!" cried Ariana, as the circle of ice they were standing on began to sink.

"We're not—Crystal can save us," gasped Rosa. "Use your freezing powers, Crystal!"

A cloud of pink sparks swirled around Crystal as she refroze the ice around them.

"No, you don't!" Ms. Willow aimed a firebolt at Crystal's head.

"Crystal!" screamed Rosa.

"Pearl—help her!" The next second, a swirling tornado of snow rose up around Crystal, hiding her from sight. With a frustrated cry, Ms. Willow

threw the firebolt at the snowstorm, where it flew past Rosa and Crystal.

Fast and furious, Ms. Willow threw more firebolts, but Pearl made the snow twister illusion bigger until all the girls and their unicorns were hidden behind it. The firebolts flashed by, exploding far behind them.

Meanwhile, Whisper started to use his magic. Skating to the edge of the snowstorm, he focused his attention on Daffodil until the little unicorn began to relax and sway.

"Pull yourself together!" screamed Ms. Willow as Daffodil rocked on her hooves beneath her.

"Whisper! That's great! Don't stop!" said Ariana as Whisper kept using his soothing magic on Daffodil. The little unicorn's eyes started to close. For a moment, it looked like she was about to fall asleep completely, but then Whisper started getting tired. Doing magic used up a lot of energy.

Ms. Willow kicked Daffodil's sides. "Stand up straight this instant!" she shouted.

With Whisper's magic fading, Daffodil obeyed Ms. Willow, raising her head and straightening her neck.

"Matilda!" Pearl gasped, breathing heavily. "I can't hold the glamour. I'm . . . I'm too tired."

The snow twister faded, revealing everyone to Ms. Willow. She stood before them, her eyes wild and her hair crackling with magic. "Now you shall all suffer for the trouble you have caused me!" She raised her hands to blast them.

"No! You're not going to hurt my friends!" whinnied Twinkle bravely. He charged at her, but his hooves slipped on the ice and he fell over. Violet was flung from his back. The island's protective magic made a bubble form around her and it set her gently on the ice before popping.

Twinkle struggled to his feet just as Ms. Willow

threw a bolt of magic at his heart. "Twinkle!"
Violet exclaimed. She leaped in front of him.

"Violet!" she heard Rosa yell in horror.

Violet shut her eyes, waiting for the bolt to
hit her, but instead she just saw a flash of light
through her closed eyelids. Her friends squealed
and Violet smelt burnt sugar. Blinking her eyes

open, she saw that the air in front of her was shimmering as it bent around her and the others like an enormous shield!

"What . . . What's happening?" said Twinkle in shock.

"It's your magic!" cried Violet. "It must be!"

Ms. Willow screamed with anger. Dismounting from Daffodil, she strode to the edge of the lagoon, her eyes fixed on the magic shield. While she was distracted, Daffodil saw her chance. She galloped past Ms. Willow and dived behind the shield with the others. Instantly, she grew taller, and her yellow-and-orange mane faded to be replaced by a splendid golden mane and tail.

"It's Prancer!" cried Matilda.

"You can use starlight to make a protective shield, Twinkle!" Prancer gasped. "I guessed you had starlight magic when you told me about your nighttime ride with Violet, and how the snow

stopped falling on you for a moment when you wanted to protect her."

Twinkle whinnied in delight just as Ms. Willow shrieked, "Prancer! Return to me right now! I command it!"

Violet expected Prancer to obey, but the unicorn didn't. Her eyes shone. "This is why I wanted to meet you in the starlight tonight, Twinkle!" she rushed on. "I hoped this would happen. When I'm protected by your starlight magic, the binding ribbons don't work and I can reveal my true form and speak freely. I've been desperate to tell someone what's been happening. I've been wanting to warn people about how evil Ms. Willow really is."

Twinkle's sides heaved as Ms. Willow threw firebolt after firebolt at the shield. "This is hard work! I don't know how long I can hold it," he panted.

Prancer looked at the others. "You need to escape and warn everyone about Ms. Willow. She's been stealing all the island's magic and storing it here in the lagoon so that she can take over the island." Ms. Willow's firebolts continued to hit the shield. "She's held a grudge against the unicorns ever since she didn't get a place at the academy when she was younger. She spent years learning dark magic. Then she stole me from my home so that she could use my spell-weaving powers. She put binding ribbons in my mane and made me disguise myself. You have to stop her. She has an evil plan to put all the unicorns on the island under her command. She—"

"I can't hold the shield any longer!" Twinkle interrupted, sinking to his knees.

"Twinkle!" cried Violet, throwing herself down beside him. "Keep trying."

But he was too tired, and Ms. Willow screamed

with delight as a bolt of magic tore through the top of the shield.

"You must leave now!" said Prancer. "Crystal, take everyone back to school in a snow twister. Tell everyone there what is going on. I'll hold Ms. Willow off. She must be stopped!"

"But what about you, Prancer?" cried Violet.

Two bolts ripped through the shield. "Don't worry about me. Just go!"

Crystal stamped her front hooves. Pink and purple sparkles swirled up from the ice and surrounded the girls and their unicorns as a snow twister rose around them. It whisked the girls and their unicorns into the air as Twinkle's starlight shield split into millions of sparkling pieces. Violet sighed in relief as they spun away, with Ms. Willow's furious screams echoing in their ears.

CHAPTER 10

Violet felt her feet hit grass, and as the sparkles cleared, she saw Unicorn Academy and heard her friends and their unicorns all talking at once. Crystal's snow twister had brought them to the lawn outside the school. Crystal hung her head, taking deep breaths, and Twinkle dropped to the ground, exhausted.

"We need to get the teachers right now!" said Matilda.

"You all go!" Violet told them. "The unicorns need sky berries to help them recover."

"We can get some, can't we, Rosa? I feel stronger already," said Crystal, who'd had her magic longer than the others. Rosa nodded and the pair left for the stables, while the others galloped off to get the teachers.

"I'm sorry I didn't have enough energy to hold the shield any longer," Twinkle said to Violet, his sides heaving. "I hope Prancer is okay."

"Me too. It must be horrible being under the control of someone like Ms. Willow, but now we'll be able to help free her. You were amazing, Twinkle. You saved us all and held the shield long enough for Prancer to tell us what's going on." Violet threw her arms around his neck. "I'm so proud of you."

Twinkle nuzzled her. "I wouldn't have found my magic if you hadn't jumped in front of me to protect me from Ms. Willow. I thought you were

going to be hurt. It was really brave of you. You shouldn't have done it, though. I'm supposed to be the one to protect you."

"No, that's wrong!" Violet said hotly. He looked at her. "We protect each other, Twinkle," she told him, more gently. "We're a team. It's not just you protecting me. We're partners."

"Partners," he said slowly, as if getting used to the idea.

Violet smiled. "Yes. So from now on, no more thinking you are the only one who has to do the protecting. And," she said, taking a deep breath—she didn't want to ruin the moment, but she knew that now was the right time to say something—"no more bossing me around all the time, okay?"

"What do you mean?" said Twinkle in surprise.

"You keep making decisions for both of us without asking what I want," Violet told him.

Twinkle thought about it. "I suppose I do." He looked at her through his eyelashes. "But if you don't want me to do that, then you need to tell me what you want, Violet. I can't read your mind."

Violet realized he was right. She'd spent so much time thinking about how bossy he was, but she was as much to blame for not speaking up. She needed to stop agreeing with him all the time, and make sure she told him what her opinion was. "Agreed," she said firmly. "From now on, we'll make decisions together. We'll be a real team."

He snorted happily. "I'd like that."

Rosa came cantering back with a bucket of sky berries. She jumped off Crystal and held the sky berries out. "Here you go, Twinkle. Eat these and you'll feel better. Oh my goodness!" She broke off with a gasp. "You've bonded!"

Violet lifted her braid and saw a strand of

purple-and-blue hair running through it. "We have! Look, Twinkle!"

Twinkle's eyes sparkled in delight. "We're going to graduate after all, Violet."

She flung her arms around him and hugged him tightly.

"Violet! Rosa!" Ms. Nettles came hurrying across the grass with Ms. Rosemary. Matilda, Ariana, and Freya followed them. "Are you and your unicorns all right?"

They nodded.

Relief crossed the teachers' faces.

"I can hardly believe Ms. Willow is behind all this," said Ms. Rosemary. She turned to Ms. Nettles. "What are we going to do?"

"We must find her and stop her," said Ms. Nettles. "We also have to free poor Prancer of the binding."

"We'll help," offered Rosa.

Ms. Nettles's strict face relaxed into a small smile. "I think you've all done quite enough for now," she said. "Thank you, Diamond dorm. You've been very brave. Now, take your unicorns back to the stables, and then off to bed, all of you. I'll arrange for some hot chocolate and cookies to be sent up to your dorm."

"Something tells me that it won't be easy to catch Ms. Willow," said Freya. Twinkle finished the sky berries and straightened up.

"I wonder what she's planning on doing," said Ariana uneasily, as Violet climbed onto Twinkle's

back. "How was she going to control all the unicorns?"

"I don't know," said Rosa. "But she has to be stopped. And if there's any way we can help, we will!"

"Hooray for Diamond dorm!" whooped Matilda, and the others joined in the cheer.

They raced back to the stables, but as the others headed inside, Twinkle stopped and looked up at the glittering sky. "I always said I liked the starlight, didn't I?" he said softly to Violet.

"You did. You said it gave you a magical feeling," said Violet. "I guess we just didn't know how true that was!" She smiled. "Starlight magic is so cool. We'll have to go for lots of nighttime rides so you can practice it."

Twinkle turned and looked at her. "One little canter before bedtime, now I've got my energy back?"

Violet grinned. "Yes, let's!"

With a happy toss of his head, Twinkle set off across the frosty grass. As the cold air stung Violet's cheeks, she buried her hands in his long mane. She urged Twinkle to go faster as the bright stars twinkled down at them from the clear night sky.

Someone is stealing all the magic
from Unicorn Island! Can Isla and Buttercup
stop them before it's too late?

Read on for a peek at the next book
in the Unicorn Academy series!

"Oh, wow! That's amazing, Matilda!" said Isla. Matilda from Diamond dorm had covered the back wall of the stables with paper and was drawing a huge mural that showed events from the last year at Unicorn Academy. There were pictures of everyone arriving on the first day, being paired with their unicorns, galloping through the grounds, and camping in the woods. The other girls from Diamond dorm—Rosa, Freya, Ariana, and Violet—were painting the background, while Unibot, the robotic unicorn that Freya built, was helping the girls by rolling around with pots of paint.

"It does look good, doesn't it?" said Rosa.

Isla nodded. "I bet the parents will love it!"

Every student who'd bonded with their unicorn—and discovered its magic power—was about to graduate. In just a few days, all the students' and unicorns' parents would come to the academy for the graduation ball. Students who weren't graduating, like Isla, would watch the ceremony, go home for Christmas, and return for a second year in January.

Matilda looked around. "Do you want to help us, Isla?"

Isla shook her head. "I'd only mess it up."

"Don't be silly. I'm no good at painting so I'm just doing the grass," said Violet. "Come and join me!"

It looked like fun, but Isla didn't want to risk ruining their beautiful mural. "It's okay," she said cheerfully, "the others from my dorm will be here soon. We're making snowflakes to hang from the ceiling." She grinned. "That's about my level when it comes to art!"

"Come and sit with us anyway," said Violet, waving Isla over with a paintbrush.

Isla smiled again. "Thanks." The Diamond

dorm girls were always so friendly to her. She was going to miss them when they all graduated.

Her own dorm, Ruby dorm, didn't get along as well as Diamond dorm. Molly and Anna were nice, but they were best friends who did everything together. The fourth member of Ruby dorm, Valentina, had rich parents who were governors at the school, and she acted like she was better than everyone else.

I wonder who will be in my dorm next year, Isla thought as she settled down to work on her snowflake. She wasn't sure how she felt about returning to the academy on her own. At least Buttercup, her confident, energetic unicorn, would be with her.

"We've been trying to think of where Ms. Willow could be hiding," said Violet. "What do you think?"

Ms. Willow had been the school nurse, until

Diamond dorm discovered that she'd been draining magic from around the island as part of an evil plan to take it over! A month ago, Ms. Willow had kidnapped Violet and her unicorn, Twinkle, and had taken them to the Frozen Lagoon where she was storing all the magic in the water under the ice. Thanks to Isla, the Diamond dorm girls had gone to Violet and Twinkle's rescue, and they'd all escaped. But Ms. Willow had vanished without a trace.

MERMICORNS

Swim into a new series!

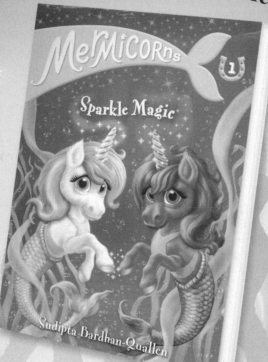

MERMICORNS

Sparkle Magic

1

Sudipta Bardhan-Quallen

Mermicorns are part unicorn, part mermaid, and totally magical!

PuRRmaids

Meet your newest feline friends!

PuRRmaids
The Scaredy Cat
1
Sudipta Bardhan-Quallen

1277a

rhcbooks.com RHCB

New friends. New adventures.
Find a new series . . . just for you!

ISADORA MOON

For ballerina and fairy and vampire lovers

MAGIC ON THE MAP

For adventurers

UNICORN ACADEMY

For unicorn lovers

PUPPY PIRATES

For dog lovers

PuRRmaids

For mermaid and cat lovers

BALLPARK Mysteries

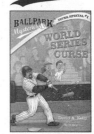

For sports fans

RHCB rhcbooks.com

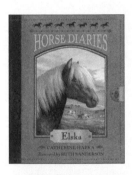

Collect all the books in the Horse Diaries series!

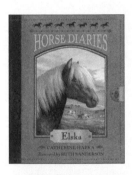

HORSE DIARIES

Elska

CATHERINE HAPKA
Illustrated by RUTH SANDERSON

HORSE DIARIES

Bell's Star

ALISON HART
Illustrated by RUTH SANDERSON

HORSE DIARIES

Koda

PATRICIA HERMES
Illustrated by RUTH SANDERSON

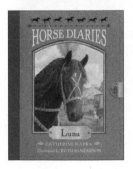

HORSE DIARIES

Luna

CATHERINE HAPKA
Illustrated by RUTH SANDERSON

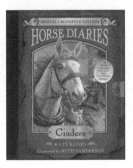

SPECIAL CROSSOVER EDITION

HORSE DIARIES

Cinders

KATE KLIMO
Illustrated by RUTH SANDERSON

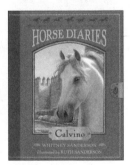

HORSE DIARIES

Calvino

WHITNEY SANDERSON
Illustrated by RUTH SANDERSON